Jeremiah Jambalaya

By Michael Newton

Illustrated by Savannah Horton

Published by Pen It! Publications, LLC in the U.S.A.
812-371-4128 www.penitpublications.com

ISBN: 978-1-952894-70-1

Illustrated by Savannah Horton

This Book Belongs To:

_____

Jeramiah Jambalaya was a little crawfish who lived with his Crawdad in a place called Big Bend Bayou.

1

Jeremiah Jambalaya didn't like living in Big Bend Bayou, because there were no other crawfish to play with.

"I want to move somewhere that I can make friends," cried Jeremiah Jambalaya to his Crawdad.

"Why can't you make friends here in Big Bend Bayou," asked Crawdad?

"There is no other crawfish living here for me to be friends with," replied Jeremiah Jambalaya.

Crawdad tried to explain to his little crawfish that he could be friends with the other creatures that lived in Big Bend Bayou, but Jeremiah Jambalaya just could not understand.

How could he be friends with someone that didn't look like him, someone that was different from him?

5

With nothing to do and no friends to play with Jeremiah Jambalaya decided to go for a swim.

Jeremiah Jambalaya was enjoying his swim when he heard crying coming from somewhere.

The little crawfish stopped swimming to look around to see if he could figure out where the crying was coming from.
He soon spotted an alligator hiding under some tree roots on the side of the bayou.

Being a curious crawfish, Jeremiah Jambalaya began swimming over to the alligator. The alligator began backing further under the tree roots.

"I heard you crying and was wondering if something was wrong," asked Jeremiah Jambalaya?

"I, I, I am just sad because nobody wants to be my friend," cried the alligator.

"Why doesn't anyone want to be your friend," Jeremiah Jambalaya asked?

There were a lot of alligators living in Big Bend Bayou, so Jeremiah Jambalaya just couldn't understand why the alligator didn't have any friends.

11

"Well, I am not like all the other alligators in the bayou. They all have sharp teeth and I don't have any teeth. I am a toothless gator. I just have big toothless gums, that is why my name is Gator Gumbo," explained Gator Gumbo.

13

Jeremiah Jambalaya thought for a moment then he realized that he had something in common with Gator Gumbo.

Just like Gator Gumbo he didn't have teeth either.

"Look at me," said Jeremiah Jambalaya, as he grinned really big.

Gator Gumbo grinned back at Jeremiah Jambalaya with a toothless smile.

Both began laughing, then they began talking about the types of games they liked to play. Both enjoyed playing hide-n-seek, tag, and going for swims around the bayou.

Jeremiah Jambalaya, however, realized something very important. The one thing they both would enjoy more than anything was having a friend.

17

With neither one of them having a friend to play with, they decided to play a game of tag together.

Gator Gumbo began chasing after Jeremiah Jambalaya trying to tag him.

The one thing about crawfish is they swim backwards and need to be on alert to their surroundings when swimming. However, Jeremiah Jambalaya was having such a good time playing with Gator Gumbo he wasn't paying attention and he swam right into something hard.

A rock?

19

"OUCH," yelled the rock.

Jeremiah Jambalaya and Gator Gumbo looked at each other, very much surprised and a bit scared.

"Jeremiah Jambalaya I have never heard a rock speak," whispered Gator Gumbo.

"Me neither," replied Jeremiah Jambalaya.

The rock began to turn around slowly. As the rock was turning around it yelled again, "I AM NOT A ROCK. I AM A TURTLE!"

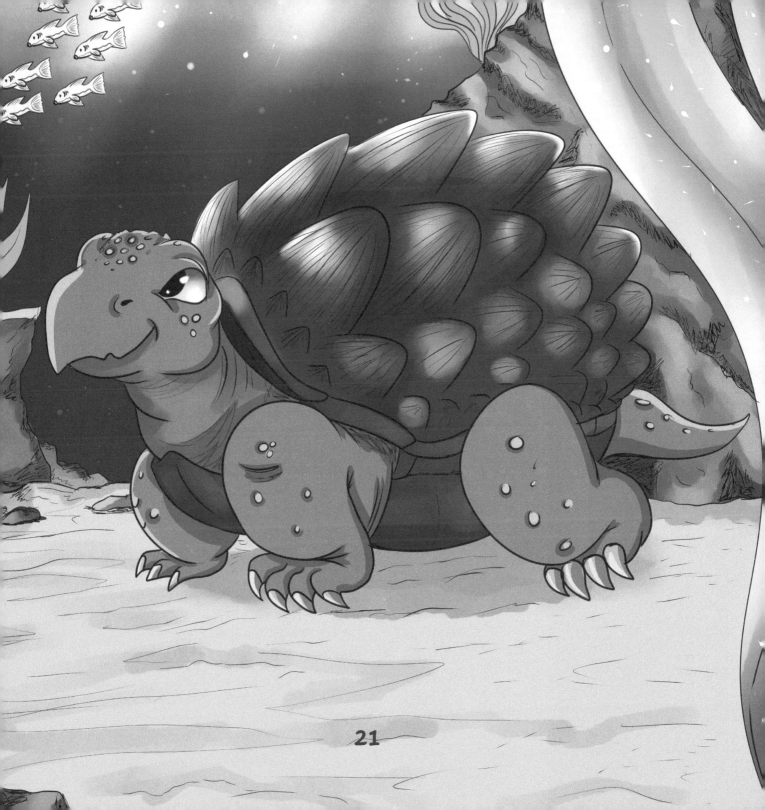

"I am so sorry I ran into you, and I am so sorry I thought you were a rock," said Jeremiah Jambalaya.

The turtle looked at Jeremiah Jambalaya then at Gator Gumbo. The turtle yelled,

"IT'S OKAY!"

Jeremiah Jambalaya and Gator Gumbo were puzzled as to why the turtle kept yelling at them if he wasn't upset with them.

"YOU ARE PROBABLY CURIOUS AS TO WHY I KEEP SNAPPING AT YOU?" the turtle replied.

Jeremiah Jambalaya and Gator Gumbo shook their heads yes; they both wondered why the turtle kept snapping at them if he wasn't upset.

"I CAN'T HELP IT I AM A SNAPPING TURTLE AND THAT IS WHAT SNAPPING

TURTLES DO!" explained the turtle.

As Jeremiah Jambalaya and Gator Gumbo talked with the turtle, he continued snapping at them when he spoke.

They learned that the turtle's name was Cypress Snapping Turtle. Just like them, Cypress Snapping Turtle had no friends.

Nobody wanted to be friends with a turtle that snapped at them every time he spoke.

They also learned that Cypress Snapping Turtle wished for friends who he could play tag, hide-n-seek, and swim around Big

Bend Bayou with.

Jeremiah Jambalaya and Gator Gumbo both knew the more who played tag or hide-n-seek together, the more fun the games would be. They decided to invite Cypress Snapping Turtle to play a game of hide-n-seek with them.

Jeremiah Jambalaya and Gator Gumbo were going to hide from Cypress Snapping Turtle, and he was going to have to find them. As Cypress Snapping Turtle began to look for them, he smiled. He was happy to have found others to play with.

As Jeremiah Jambalaya was searching for a hiding place, he began thinking about how he had many things in common with Gator Gumbo and Cypress Snapping Turtle.

He thought about how they all enjoyed playing the same games, swimming around the bayou, and of course, how they all wanted a friend. He wondered if his Crawdad could be right, that he could be friends with someone different than him.

Jeremiah Jambalaya found a tree limb lying on the bottom of the bayou that he thought would be a good hiding place. However, it didn't take long before Cypress Snapping Turtle found him.

"I FOUND YOU!" snapped Cypress Snapping Turtle.

They both laughed at how poorly Jeremiah was hidden. It felt good to have someone to laugh with. They decided to split up to find Gator Gumbo.

Jeremiah Jambalaya noticed that on the bottom of the bayou was a mud pit. He also noticed something was hiding in the mud.

'It had to be Gator Gumbo,' thought Jeremiah Jambalaya, so he decided to quietly sneak up on him.

As soon as Jeremiah Jambalaya was within reach, he gently touched who he thought was Gator Gumbo with his claw and yelled, "I found you!"

"I found you," repeated a strange voice.

Out of the mud popped up a snake.

Jeremiah Jambalaya jumped back, not knowing if the snake would harm him. He looked at the snake and said, "Sorry I didn't mean to disturb you."

"Sorry I didn't mean to disturb you," mocked the snake.

Jeremiah Jambalaya wondered why the
snake would think that she disturbed him.

"My friends and I were playing a game, and
I thought you were one of my friends.
So, I actually disturbed you," explained
Jeremiah Jambalaya.

The snake smiled at Jeremiah Jambalaya and then repeated, "My friends and I were play-ing a game, and I thought you were one of my friends. So, I actually disturbed you."

Then the snake began crying, which confused Jeremiah Jambalaya. The little crawfish couldn't understand why the snake was mocking everything he said or why she had started crying.

Gator Gumbo and Cypress Snapping Turtle heard all the commotion, so they stopped playing to to find out what was going on.

When the snake finally stopped crying, she explained to everyone that she couldn't help but mock them. She is a water moccasin and that is what water moccasins do; they repeat or mock everything others say.

"Nobody wants to be friends with someone who mocks them," said the water moccasin.

43

Jeremiah Jambalaya thought to himself that everyone needs a friend, even if they have annoying habits.

"What is your name?" Jeremiah Jambalaya asked the snake.

"What is your name?" mocked the snake.

"My name is Jeremiah Jambalaya," replied the crawfish.

"My name is Jeremiah Jambalaya," mocked the snake.

45

Gator Gumbo and Cypress Snapping Turtle
tried to introduce themselves and, of course,
the snake mocked them, as well.

The snake was afraid that she was annoying
them, and that they would leave without
giving her a chance to be their friend.

Finally, the snake stopped mocking them
long enough to apologize and let them know
her name was Missy Water Moccasin.

Jeremiah Jambalaya, Gator Gumbo, and Cypress Snapping Turtle learned that Missy Water Moccasin enjoyed the same games as they did. Like them, the one thing she really wanted was a friend.

The problem was, they had trouble talking with Missy Water Moccasin because she mocked everything they would say.

However, they all knew how important it was for them to have friends, so they wanted to give Missy Water Moccasin a chance to have a friend too.

Then Jeremiah Jambalaya had an idea!

What if Missy Water Moccasin was to hold her tongue between her lips when someone was talking. He thought that maybe it would keep her from mocking others.

Missy Water Moccasin agreed to give it a try and it worked. They were able to have normal conversations without being mocked.

The four new friends spent the rest of the
day playing and talking together.

Occasionally Missy Water Moccasin would
forget to hold her tongue, but nobody
seemed to mind, and it gave them all
a good laugh.

53

When it was time for everyone to go home, they decided they would meet the next day at the roots of the tree where Jeremiah Jambalaya first met Gator Gumbo.

They even decided to name the tree the Friendship Tree. It would be their own special place.

When Jeremiah Jambalaya got home,
he told his Crawdad all about his day and
his new friends.

"I finally understand how I can be friends
with someone who doesn't look like me and
is different than me," said Jeremiah
Jambalaya to his Crawdad.

57

"Even if we are different and don't look the same on the outside, we all have a lot more in common on the inside, don't we Crawdad?" asked the little crawfish.

Proud of his little crawfish, Crawdad looked at Jeremiah Jambalaya with a big smile, and simply replied, "Yes."

59

Jeremiah Jambalaya fell fast asleep that
night thinking about his new friends, the fun
day they had, and knowing that together,
the new friends were going to have many
more adventures.

61

The End

Author Michael Newton lives in a small rural town in the beautiful Missouri Ozarks with his wife Rhonda, and two sons Braden and Logan.

Michael received his Bachelor of Science in Nursing degree from the University of Missouri-Columbia.

Michael has worked in many areas of nursing as a registered nurse and currently has the honor to work and care for real life hero's our American veterans.

Recently Michael has began writing stories including stories from characters that he remembers from his childhood imagination. *JEREMIAH JAMBALAYA* is his first book to be published.

Along with writing Michael enjoys photography, traveling, and most of all spending time with his family.

CPSIA information can be obtained
at www.ICGtesting.com
Printed in the USA
LVHW070232010820
662068LV00021B/1067